DINOSAUR COVE™

CLASH OF THE MONSTER CROCS

by
REX STONE

illustrated by
MIKE SPOOR

Series created by
Working Partners Ltd

With special thanks to Jane Clarke
For my adventurous sons, Andrew and Robert. R.S.

Everyone at the Dromkeen Gallery, Australia,
for making a UK Illustrator feel so welcome. M.S.

OXFORD
UNIVERSITY PRESS

Great Clarendon Street, Oxford OX2 6DP
Oxford University Press is a department of the University of Oxford.
It furthers the University's objective of excellence in research, scholarship,
and education by publishing worldwide in

Oxford   New York

Auckland   Cape Town   Dar es Salaam   Hong Kong   Karachi
Kuala Lumpur   Madrid   Melbourne   Mexico City   Nairobi
New Delhi   Shanghai   Taipei   Toronto

With offices in

Argentina   Austria   Brazil   Chile   Czech Republic   France   Greece
Guatemala   Hungary   Italy   Japan   Poland   Portugal   Singapore
South Korea   Switzerland   Thailand   Turkey   Ukraine   Vietnam

Oxford is a registered trade mark of Oxford University Press
in the UK and in certain other countries

© Working Partners Limited 2010
Illustrations © Mike Spoor 2010
Eye logo © Dominic Harman 2010

Data available
ISBN: 978-0-19-272977-4

1 3 5 7 9 10 8 6 4 2

Printed in Great Britain by CPI Cox and Wyman, Reading, Berkshire
Paper used in the production of this book is a natural,
recyclable product made from wood grown in sustainable forests
The manufacturing process conforms to the environmental
regulations of the country of origin

FACT FILE

▷ JAMIE'S DAD'S MUSEUM ON THE BOTTOM FLOOR OF THE LIGHTHOUSE IN DINOSAUR COVE IS THE SECOND BEST PLACE IN THE WORLD TO BE. THE FIRST IS DINO WORLD, OF COURSE, THE SECRET THAT JAMIE AND HIS BEST FRIEND TOM HAVE DISCOVERED IN THE BACK OF A DEEP, DARK CAVE. BUT THEY HAVE TO BE CAREFUL. IT'S NOT EASY TO OUTRUN A HUNGRY DINOSAUR!

JAMIE

- **FULL NAME:** JAMIE MORGAN
- **AGE:** 8 YEARS
- **SIZE:** 1 JATOM*
- **TOP SPEED:** 10 KPH
- **LIKES:** FOSSIL HUNTING AND LEARNING ABOUT DINOSAURS
- **DISLIKES:** BEING STUCK INDOORS

Jamie's eye

Jamie's foot

Jamie's hand

*NOTE: A JATOM IS THE SIZE OF JAMIE OR TOM: 125 CM TALL AND 27 KG IN WEIGHT

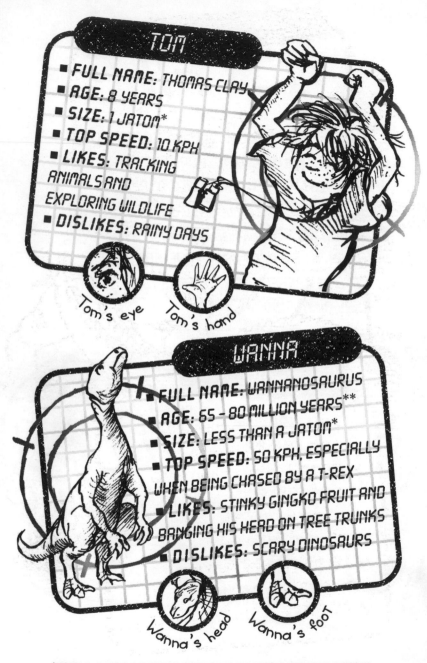

TOM

- **FULL NAME:** THOMAS CLAY
- **AGE:** 8 YEARS
- **SIZE:** 1 JATOM*
- **TOP SPEED:** 10 KPH
- **LIKES:** TRACKING ANIMALS AND EXPLORING WILDLIFE
- **DISLIKES:** RAINY DAYS

Tom's eye

Tom's hand

WANNA

- **FULL NAME:** WANNANOSAURUS
- **AGE:** 65 – 80 MILLION YEARS**
- **SIZE:** LESS THAN A JATOM*
- **TOP SPEED:** 50 KPH, ESPECIALLY WHEN BEING CHASED BY A T-REX
- **LIKES:** STINKY GINGKO FRUIT AND BANGING HIS HEAD ON TREE TRUNKS
- **DISLIKES:** SCARY DINOSAURS

Wanna's head

Wanna's foot

*NOTE: A JATOM IS THE SIZE OF JAMIE OR TOM: 125 CM TALL AND 27 KG IN WEIGHT
**NOTE: SCIENTISTS CALL THIS PERIOD THE LATE CRETACEOUS

POSTOSUCHUS

Postosuchus's eye

Postosuchus's teeth

Postosuchus's foot

Postosuchus's scales

- **FULL NAME:** POSTOSUCHUS
- **AGE:** 230 MILLION YEARS***
- **HEIGHT WHEN REARING UP:** 3 JATOMS*
- **LENGTH:** 4 JATOMS*
- **WEIGHT:** 25 JATOMS*
- **LIKES:** RUNNING FAST AND PLAYING SNAP
- **DISLIKES:** MEALS THAT GET AWAY

*NOTE: A JATOM IS THE SIZE OF JAMIE OR TOM: 125 CM TALL AND 27 KG IN WEIGHT
***NOTE: SCIENTISTS CALL THIS PERIOD THE EARLY TRIASSIC

Landslips where clay and fossils are

Muddy beach

DINO CAVE

High Tide beach line

Low Tide beach line

Sea

Smuggler's Point

9

'THE DAWN OF THE DINOSAURS!' Jamie
Morgan finished writing the capital letters in
felt pen, then fixed the banner to the wall of
his dad's museum in Dinosaur Cove. Beneath
the banner was a table-top model of a
prehistoric landscape with a forest, a swamp,
and a dried-out river bed snaking across it.

'Triassic Corner looks awesome!' Jamie's
best friend Tom Clay said proudly. He and
Jamie had spent ages making the landscape
model using crumpled newspaper and lots of

THE DAWN OF

glue and paint. Tom picked up
the cardboard cut-out of a pig-like reptile
he had just finished working on.

'Two hundred and thirty million years ago
fearsome Triassic monsters walked the land . . . '
Tom said in his wildlife commentator voice.
'The burrowing lystrosaurus lived in deep
holes . . . ' He glued his cardboard model
to the dried-up river bed that wound down
the model landscape. ' . . . then came the
first dinosaurs. The long–
necked plateosaurus . . . '

THE DINOSAURS!

Tom placed a cut-out of the Triassic's biggest plant-eating dinosaur at the edge of the swamp.

'Hunted by the vicious eoraptor!' Jamie interrupted, sticking his model of the meat eater between the papier mâché bushes at the edge of the swamp.

'Hey!' Tom said. 'I don't want your eoraptor eating my plateosaurus.'

'That's life, you wombat!' Jamie laughed.
'Hey, Dad,' he called. 'Come and see! We've
finished Triassic Corner.'

Mr Morgan was signing some papers for a
delivery man who was standing at the front
door of the old lighthouse with a huge
wooden crate on a hand-trolley.

'Wheel it over, please,' he told the delivery
man, then he headed towards the boys.
'Great job!' he said, putting on his
glasses to study the boys'
work. 'I like the tiny
Triassic frog.

FRAGILE

The Lighthouse
Dinosaur Cove Museum
Dinosaur Cove

DINOSAUR BONES

And the dried-up river bed shows how hot it was in the Triassic. You've really done your research.'

Tom nudged Jamie and they shared a private smile. They knew a lot about the Triassic because they had visited it, *and* other prehistoric time periods. Finding the entrance to Dino World, a world of amazing living, breathing prehistoric beasts, was their top Dinosaur Cove secret!

'And you finished the landscape just in time,' Mr Morgan went on, lifting the lid of the wooden crate. 'Our star Triassic fossil has arrived!'

Jamie and Tom peered inside. Nestling in shredded cardboard was a massive skull with a long jaw full of dagger-like teeth resting on top of a pile of fossilized bones.

'Meet the king of the Triassic world,'
Jamie's dad announced. 'The number one
Triassic predator: Postosuchus!'

'It looks like a humongous crocodile,' Tom
breathed.

'Postosuchus's skull is crocodilian,' Mr
Morgan agreed. 'But it had long legs to run
down its prey. Some scientists call it the
"running crocodile".'

16

'Awesome!' Jamie exclaimed, pulling out a bone that was as long as his arm. It felt smooth and very heavy.

'A complete skeleton like this is very rare,' his dad told him, taking the bone from Jamie. 'I'll need peace and quiet while I work out how to assemble it . . . '

'No problem,' Jamie and Tom said together. 'We're going out!'

Jamie grabbed his backpack.

'Let's find some real live postoes!' he said excitedly.

'Got the Triassic ammonite?' Tom asked him.

'Check!' Jamie said. The fossil that was the key to the Triassic Dino World was safely in his bag.

The two friends raced out of the museum, down the cliff steps and along the sandy beach

towards the far headland. They scrambled up
the rocks to the old smuggler's cave at
Smuggler's Point and squeezed through the hole
at the back to the dark secret cave beyond.

Jamie snapped on his torch and placed his
foot in the first of the five fossil dinosaur

footprints that led across the floor to an apparently solid rock wall. His heart leapt with excitement as he counted the footprints.

'One, two, three, four . . . five!'

In a blinding flash of light, he was in Dino World again, standing in fresh dinosaur footprints in the hollowed-out trunk of an ancient tree.

'Five!' Tom was right behind him.

Jamie stepped out of the shade and doubled over as the hot, thin Triassic air took his breath away. Giant insects were whirring and buzzing above his head.

Something scraped
the back of his hand.
Something rough and wet.

'Wanna!' Jamie gasped. 'You made me jump!'

The little dinosaur stopped licking Jamie's
hand and wagged his tail. Then he bounded
up to Tom, spitting out pine needles as he
grunked for joy.

'Wanna's been having a snack while he
waited for us,' Tom laughed. 'He's already
acclimatized!'

'Great to see you're ready for
our next adventure, Wanna!'
Jamie straightened up as he
got his breath back, and
patted their little
wannanosaurus friend
on his bony head.
Wanna was from the
Cretaceous, but he

was always there, like magic, to join them, whatever time period they came out in.

Jamie and Tom shaded their eyes from the glaring sun and scanned the shimmering Triassic landscape. All around them, tree-ferns and conifer trees encrusted with orange lichens towered over a jungle of waist-high ferns.

'Now,' said Jamie. 'Where do postoes live?'

'Crocodiles live in water, so that's a good place to start looking for postoes,' Tom said, delving into his back pocket and pulling out the map he had made of Triassic World on their last visit. 'It's too dry here.' He studied the map. 'The ponds we saw are over to the east.'

Jamie took out his compass and checked the bearing.

'This way,' he said, plunging into the forest, pushing aside the broad leaf ferns. The ground became damper underfoot, and vines

began to festoon the
tree-ferns and
conifers. They trekked
on, past a weird slimy
blood-red fungus sprouting
from a dead tree trunk. Now, the Triassic

jungle was thicker and darker and spooky shadows flitted from tree to tree as they passed. Something like a woodlouse, as long as his forearm and with loads of little legs, scuttled over Jamie's foot. He jumped backwards in alarm.

'It's only a millipede, you wombat,'
Tom laughed, as the shiny silvery-
grey creature burrowed
into the leaf mould.
'It'd be awesome
to have one of
those for a pet.'
'What would you
feed it on?' Jamie asked him.
'Young leaves, like thïs one.' Tom reached
out to pick the spiral shoot of an emerald
green fern.

'Aaah!' Tom screamed, flapping his hand
about. 'It moved!'

The fern frond landed on the ground.
Wanna sniffed at it, then sneezed violently
and jumped backwards as it began to crawl
away.

'It's only a stick insect, fossil brains!' Jamie
chuckled. 'That'd make a cool pet, too.'

'Shhh!' Tom
whispered, putting his
binoculars to his eyes.
'There's a lizard up ahead.
Don't scare it away, there's
something weird about it . . .'

Jamie shaded his eyes. A blue-green lizard
with an orange back, the size of an iguana,
was sunning itself on the gnarly root of a
conifer tree.

'Do you see what I see?' Tom handed Jamie
the binoculars.

Jamie sucked in his breath in surprise.
What he'd thought were orange scales looked
like two rows of spiky orange feathers, folded
flat along the creature's back.

'It's a flying dinosaur!' Jamie breathed.

The lizard turned towards Jamie and raised its feathers like a double fan.

'You know what this means?' Tom grabbed the binoculars. 'Scientists say that archaeopteryx was the first bird. But that's from the Jurassic, zillions of years later . . . '

'We must have made a new dinosaur discovery!' Jamie pulled the Fossil Finder out of his backpack and waited for the '*HAPPY*

HUNTING' message to appear on
the screen. Then he hastily
typed in '*TRIASSIC. LITTLE
DINOSAUR. FEATHERS.*'

A picture popped up.

'It's a longisquama,' he
told Tom. He began reading
from the screen. '*THE CURIOUS FEATHER-
LIKE STRUCTURES WERE NOT USED FOR FLIGHT. THEY
WERE MERELY VERY LONG SCALES USED BY THE
ANIMAL TO COOL ITSELF DOWN.*'

The longisquama lowered its long orange
spiky scales and sauntered slowly up the tree
root. They watched it claw its way up the
conifer's trunk and disappear among the thick
pine needles.

'We didn't make an important scientific
discovery after all,' Tom sighed as Jamie
stowed the Fossil Finder in his backpack, and
took out his compass again.

Grunk?

Wanna peered hopefully into Jamie's backpack.

'No gingkoes in there this time, Wanna,' Jamie told him.

Tom looked at the little dinosaur.

'You know, we may not have found a new flying dinosaur, but we've discovered much more about the wannanosaurus than scientists have,' he told Jamie. 'I've never seen a dinosaur book that says they grunk and their favourite food is stinky gingko fruits.'

'And only we get to see it just like it really was,' Jamie agreed, setting the compass on a flat tree root to get an accurate reading. 'This way,' he said, hoisting up his backpack and setting off once more. 'Imagine how confused scientists would be if they found Wanna's footprints in Triassic rocks!'

'You know what would confuse future scientists the most?' Tom said behind him.

'Finding human bones in fossil dinosaur dung?' Jamie suggested, flashing Tom a grin over his shoulder.

'Finding a fossilized compass, you wombat!' Tom pointed to the compass Jamie had left behind.

Jamie picked up the compass and popped it into his pocket.

An eerie low-pitched call echoed through the trees.

U-wak, u-wak! Waaaak!

Wanna cocked his head to one side.

'It sounds like a cross between a giant zombie frog and a vampire duck,' Jamie said, shivering.

'Crocodiles sound a bit like that,' Tom said, nervously. 'I think it might be postoes. We must be close to the pond.'

They pushed through the vine-festooned trees towards a dense clump of high horsetail ferns.

U-wak!

The call was closer, now. Wanna shifted from foot to foot.

Ahead, Jamie saw a flash of sunlight glinting on water.

'The pond's just the other side of those horsetails!' he told them.

'We're hunting the top Triassic predator,' Tom murmured

nervously. 'What if it decides that we're on the menu?'

'Dad said the posto is called the running crocodile,' Jamie reminded him.

'It's not called the climbing crocodile.' He pointed to a huge old tree growing between the horsetails at the edge of the pond. The tree's root system spread out like giant arthritic fingers and its heavy branches hung over the water, trailing thick jungle vines. 'This looks like a good tree to climb.'

'Great idea!' Tom agreed. 'We should be safe up there.'

CHAPTER 3

The boys and Wanna raced each other to the
big old tree at the edge of the pond. The
highest branches were festooned with trailing
vines and drooped with the weight of juicy
ripe fruit. There was a familiar smell in the
air. A cross between baby sick and rotting
meat. Wanna snuffled deeply. Slimy dino
drool began to plop on Jamie's foot.

'It's a stinky gingko tree!' Jamie exclaimed.

Wanna stood as if rooted to the spot in
amazement.

'It's the biggest gingko tree he's ever seen.' Tom chuckled. He grabbed hold of a trailing vine and gave it a couple of sharp tugs. Jamie did the same.

'And the stinkiest.' Jamie gagged as, hand over hand, they pulled themselves up on the vines, walking their feet up the tree trunk.

Wanna tried to copy them, but it was no good. The little dinosaur's clawed hands and feet could not get a grip. The boys watched in amusement as, time after time, he launched himself onto a vine, scrabbled wildly, then slithered back down to the ground, grunking sadly.

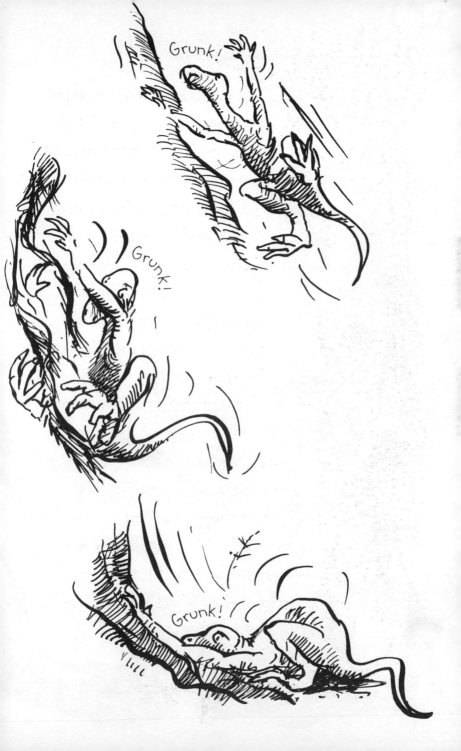

'I'll get him.' Jamie abseiled back down
and patted his backpack. 'Hop on, Wanna.'
The little dinosaur hooked his hands and
feet onto Jamie's backpack and clung on.
It was a struggle to haul them both up the
vine, and Tom had to lean down and
help pull Wanna on to a sturdy branch
that grew out over the pond. Wanna

craned his neck and dribbled at the clusters of ripe gingko fruit at the end of the branch.

'We'll get a good view of the water from here,' Tom said. He swung a leg either side of the branch and began to edge along it.

Grunk!

Wanna followed Tom, his eyes fixed firmly on the gingko fruit. Jamie brought up the rear. They swung their legs and bumped over the vines that were wrapped around the branch.

'This would make an awesome rope swing,' Jamie commented, tugging on one of the vines that trailed down over the pond.

'Yeah, right. You first,' Tom joked.

They carried on until the branch began to dip towards the pond.

'We can't go any further,' Tom said, shuffling backwards and blocking Wanna's progress. 'Gross!' he exclaimed as Wanna slobbered down his T-shirt.

'We'd better pick him some gingkoes before he drowns us in drool,' Jamie said. He settled the little dinosaur in a bowl-shaped knot in the thick branch. Then he carefully stretched up and plucked a handful of smelly, squishy gingko fruit for Wanna to munch.

The little dinosaur grunked happily and began to slurp up his disgusting snack.

Tom scanned the murky water with his binoculars.

'Something's down there,' he said. 'See the ripples near that rotting stump of a tree trunk

in the centre of the pond?' Tom leaned around
Wanna and handed the binoculars to Jamie.

Jamie wrapped his legs tightly round the
branch and focused on the ripples. They were
radiating out from what looked like four
floating tennis balls, covered in chocolate-
brown scales. Jamie's heart skipped a beat as

he realized what they were. The hooded eyes
of a pair of postoes! He could just make out
their long snouts and brown-green scaly
armoured bodies, the length of a school bus,
floating immediately below the surface. One
was an arm's length bigger than the other,

with a
broader skull.

'Postoes!' Jamie breathed,
passing the binoculars around Wanna,
so that Tom could take them. Wanna stopped
chomping and looked curiously at Tom, his
last gingko clamped firmly in his jaws.

'Those armoured scales on their backs look
like tree bark,' Tom whispered, staring down

into the pond. 'Postoes are camouflaged to look like floating tree trunks so they can lie in wait for their prey!'

Wanna leaned over to see what they were looking at.

'Careful, Wanna!' Jamie grabbed hold of the little dinosaur. Wanna spat out his last gingko in surprise. The fruit dropped into the pond below with a *Plop!*

The postoes' heads darted towards the sound. Then they glided through the water.

'They think it's the sound of prey falling into the water!' Tom whispered to Jamie. He reached up for another gingko fruit. Wanna looked at him hopefully,

but Tom threw the gingko into the water
behind the postoes.

The murky water foamed as the
postoes whipped round, thrashing
their long scaly tails and
snapping their
fearsome jaws.

Great
ripples of
water spread
out as they fiercely
jostled each other to be first to get
to the place where the splash had come from.

'Wow! They're fast!' Tom commented. 'That was some competition. Did you see those teeth?'

'Awesome! Like daggers!' Jamie agreed, watching the postoes settle down. The two monster crocs lurked in the water, as still as logs, ignoring the ripe gingko fruit that bobbed around them.

Beside him, Wanna peered down into the water.

'Wanna wants the gingkoes!' Tom said. 'No! Don't lean over, Wanna . . . '

Gr-u-u-u-nk!

With a stab of alarm, Jamie whirled round. The little dinosaur was upside down, his feet gripping the vines on the branch and his limbs flailing wildly. His long toes were losing their grip.

'Wanna!'

The little dinosaur hurtled towards the pond.

'Oh no!' Tom gasped. 'He can't swim!'

Wanna hit the brown water with a

Splosh!

Two sets of beady crocodilian eyes turned

towards him . . .

CHAPTER 4

SEARCH:
A B C D E F G H I J K L M N
O P Q R S T U V W X Y Z
1 2 3 4 5 6 7 8 9 0

'He's lunch!' Jamie wailed, peering into the murky water.

Wanna bobbed to the surface. Jamie held his breath as the little dinosaur clawed himself up on to the stump of rotten wood in the middle of the pond. Jamie breathed a sigh of relief.

The little wannanosaurus looked around desperately.

Grunkkkk! Grunkkkk!

The cloudy brown water immediately in front of the postoes' eyes had begun to bubble

as if it was boiling. Two sets of scaly nostrils flared out of the murk.

Furff! Furff!

'The postoes have realized that something tastier than a gingko fruit has just fallen into their pond!' Tom said grimly.

The boys watched as the monstrous crocs sped towards the wannanosaurus, parting the

Furff! Furff!

water like speedboats. Wanna
lowered his bony head and
scrambled back, trembling.
He stepped onto a piece of rotten
wood, but it snapped free of the
ancient tree stump and he almost
fell back into the pond.

'He's croc food, for sure.' Tom gulped.
'There's nowhere for him to hide!'

Tom covered his eyes as the bigger posto
opened its powerful jaws full of slicing teeth.

Jamie's heart felt as if it was turning to
ice. He was frozen to the spot. Then, when
it seemed that Wanna would be gobbled
whole, the second posto reared
out of the water. It heaved itself
onto its companion's back,
scrabbling at it with its clawed
feet, and pushing it under the
boggy water.

The
big one
thrashed its tail
and rolled
violently, giving
Jamie a flash of its
yellow striped underbelly.

'They're fighting over who eats Wanna!'
Jamie cried.

Tom peered out from between his fingers.
'Crocodiles roll like that to tear chunks of
flesh off their prey,' he said, lowering his
hands.

Jamie's mind was racing
as he stared down at the
gigantic crocodiles thrashing,
snapping, and flailing. It was
only a matter of time before the
postoes stopped fighting each other
and the winner turned on Wanna.
His little dinosaur friend was still
clinging on to the rotten tree
trunk, shaking from snout to
tail. He had to move, and fast!

Jamie scrambled along the branch of
the gingko tree until he was directly above
the little dinosaur. Then he grabbed hold of
a trailing vine, and gave it a tug.

'Go, Jamie!' Tom yelled.

Wanna looked up, hopefully.

Hand over hand, Jamie slithered down the
vine. He could only hope that the monster
crocs were too busy fighting to notice him.

CHAPTER 5

Jamie dropped down onto the rotten tree stump, taking care not to let go of the vine.

Wanna leapt onto his backpack and clung on. Jamie's arm muscles strained as, sweating and panting, he struggled to pull them both up the vine.

Swoosh!

A brown wave bucketed over them. Jamie shot a glance at the huge postoes. They were still wrestling with each other, churning the murky water into foam.

'Help pull us up, Tom!'
he yelled.

Tom heaved on the
vine, slowly hauling
Jamie and Wanna
towards the gingko tree.

Waaak!
Waaak!

There was a horrible
roaring beneath them.
Jamie gripped the
vine so hard that his
knuckles went white.
The postoes had
noticed that their
lunch was getting
away!

'Grub's off!' Jamie
yelled at them.

The bigger posto reared towards him. Quick as a flash, Jamie swung his legs to dodge its ferocious teeth. The posto's jaws closed on empty air with a *snap!* It fell back into the pond, keeping its eyes on its swinging target.

The second posto rose up out of the water. Jamie hung on to the vine and thrashed his legs so that they swung out of the way of its snapping jaws.

Grunk, grunk, grunk!

Jamie could feel the little dinosaur shaking with fear as they swung on the vine, above the ferocious postoes. Each time they came within range, the monstrous crocs snatched at Jamie's feet. He kicked wildly, making the swing of the vine arc wider and wider across the pond. It made a creaky, squeaky noise as the top of the vine rubbed against the branch that Tom was sitting on.

'Stop swinging!' Tom yelled. 'The vine's breaking!'

'I can't stop it!' Jamie screamed. There was a ripping sound and the vine snapped at the end of the arc. He could feel Wanna lose his grip on the backpack as they tumbled through the air and hit the water with two loud sploshes.

'Gross!' Jamie gagged, sitting up and spitting out a mouthful of warm pond water that tasted as if someone had boiled rotting cabbages and slugs in it. His hands and feet were deep in the slimy gloop at the bottom of the pond.

Jamie struggled to stand up, looking round wildly to see if Wanna was OK. The little dinosaur was already on his feet. As fast as they could, Jamie and Wanna scrambled through the stinking muck. Jamie glanced behind. A cold shiver ran down his spine. The postoes had turned their way.

'Don't stop!' Tom yelled, grabbing a vine

and abseiling down the tree. He raced towards
his friends, leaping the giant tree roots.

'Take my hand!' Tom pulled first Wanna,
then Jamie, through the horsetails, out onto
dry land at the edge of the pond. Then he
looked over Jamie's and Wanna's shoulders
towards the water. Jamie saw the blood drain
from his friend's face.

Waaak! Waaak!
The postoes hunting cry was so close
now, it was almost deafening.

'Run!' Tom gasped.

CHAPTER 6

The three friends raced through the Triassic
jungle, leaping over ferns and dodging conifer
trunks and horsetails.

Behind them, they could hear the monster
crocs crashing through the undergrowth.

'We'll never make it!' Tom gasped,
ducking under a low branch. 'The postoes are
bulldozing their way through.'

Jamie glanced over his shoulder as they
clambered across the huge tangled roots of
an enormously tall conifer. The postoes damp

scales glimmered like melted chocolate in the
hot sunshine. Their pointed snouts and long
armoured bodies were cutting through the
dense undergrowth as they sped towards their
prey, powered by their long hind legs.

'Now I know why they're called running crocodiles,' Jamie panted.

'They're gaining on us,' Tom groaned, as they heaved themselves over another root, disturbing a longisquama. The longisquama scuttled up the tree trunk and stopped a metre or so above their heads, clinging to the bark.

'Can we get up this tree?' Tom asked.

'Not unless we're longisquamas.' Jamie looked up at the bare trunk of the huge conifer in despair. There were no low branches or trailing vines to help them climb it.

Waak! Waak!

The postoes were so close, Jamie could hear them crashing through the undergrowth behind them.

Grunk!

Wanna ducked down between the tree roots.

'Wanna's got the right idea,' Tom whispered. 'The postoes might not spot us if we keep really still.'

They squeezed into a gloomy gap between the roots.

Jamie looked up to see the postoes yellow-striped bellies as they hurdled over their hiding place. He peered out between the tree roots, hoping the monstrous predators had run on. But as he watched, they skidded to a halt. The postoes' nostrils flared as they turned their heads and sniffed the air.

Furff, furrff!

The prehistoric crocodiles were trying to pick up their scent. The boys and

Wanna huddled closer together in their hiding place among the tree roots.

'This doesn't look good,' Jamie breathed.

'We need to distract them,' Tom whispered urgently. 'Throw something to confuse them!'

'Like in the pond!' Jamie agreed, looking round for something to throw. 'No gingkoes here. Or stones, or even a twig . . . '

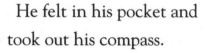

He felt in his pocket and took out his compass.

'You can't throw that!' Tom hissed. 'If we lost it, it could get fossilized, remember?'

Jamie glanced back at the postoes. They were slinking closer, sniffing the ground. He could smell the pond-stink on them.

'There's no choice if we want to stay alive,' he whispered, grimly.

Jamie gripped the compass like a baseball, and swept his arm backwards, ready to pitch.

A strange cry of alarm rang through the
Triassic forest.

Taga-taga-taga-taga!

Jamie paused, his hand raised in the air.
The sound had come from above them.
The boys craned their necks to look up.
There, on the tree trunk, was the longisquama.
It was staring angrily at the postoes!

Taga-taga-taga-taga!

The two rows of spiky orange feather-like
scales on its back
were raised.

Taga-Taga-Taga-Taga!

Taga-Taga-Taga-Taga!

'It's toast!' Tom breathed.

The boys watched as the longisquama opened its two feathery fans and launched itself off the branch. It brushed the end of a postoes snout as it soared into the trees.

Waaak! Waak!

The posto raced off after the longisquama, snapping its jaws with its companion lumbering after it.

'It's not just gliding; it *can* fly!' Jamie breathed as they watched the longisquama flap away from the postoes on its fan-like orange wings.

'We did make a discovery after all.' Tom said with a grin.

The longisquama and the postoes disappeared into the undergrowth. Jamie,

Tom, and Wanna listened to the crashing sounds die away. From the distance, there came two muffled but distinct sploshes.

'Phew! The postoes have gone back home,' Jamie murmured. 'I think we should, as well!'

'That was too close for comfort,' Tom agreed, as they jogged back to the safety of the hollow tree. Wanna grunked with relief as soon as he saw it.

Waaak!
Waak!

Sluuurp!

Jamie bent down so his face was on a level with Wanna's. 'Sorry you nearly got eaten, Wanna,' he said. The little dinosaur bobbed his bony head.

Sluuurp!

His sandpapery tongue left a trail of dino drool across Jamie's nose. Then he bounded up to Tom and licked his hand.

'I think he forgives us!' Tom laughed, wiping his sticky fingers on his T-shirt.

'It's time to go now, Wanna,' Jamie told him. 'See you later, alligator!'

Wanna wagged his tail and dived into the hollowed out tree trunk. Tom and Jamie watched as he disappeared.

'Ready, Jamie?' Tom asked.

 72

Jamie nodded and carefully placed his feet into the muddy prints and began walking backwards.

In the blink of an eye, the footprints turned to stone and he was back in the secret cave in Dinosaur Cove, with Tom right behind him. They emerged onto the headland of Smuggler's Point.

Tom looked down at the sea.

'The tide's coming in!' he exclaimed. 'Quick!'

They scrambled down to the beach and splashed through the salty water, then climbed the cliff steps to the lighthouse museum.

Jamie's dad looked round from his work
as they barged through the door in their
soaking clothes.

'Been messing about in the water?' he asked
absent-mindedly.

The boys shared a secret smile.

'Come and see our new postosuchus.'
Mr Morgan beckoned them over to Triassic
Corner. 'I've almost finished mounting it.
It must have been a fearsome beast.'

The postosuchus skeleton was rearing high
up on its back legs, snapping at the air, just
like the real ones had done.

'Awesome!' Tom and Jamie said together.

'I tried to make it look as lifelike as
possible,' Jamie's dad told them.

Tom and Jamie grinned at
each other.

'It is very, *very* lifelike!'
they agreed.

DINOSAUR WORLD

BOYS' ROUTE

Desert

Oasis

Fertile river

Ocean That way

Red Mountain

Forest

Dried out river bed

Cave in
Rotten Tree

Pond

Scrubland

GLOSSARY

Archaeopteryx (ar-kee-op-ter-ix) – the earliest bird capable of flight, with sharp teeth, three clawed fingers, and a long bony tail. Archaeopteryx was not a fussy feeder, eating small animals, plants and insects.

Eoraptor (ee-oh-rap-tor) – a small, lightly built dinosaur with hollow bones, much like today's birds. It stood on two legs and was a speedy runner, using its clawed arms to grasp its prey of lizards and worms.

Longisquama (long-is-karm-ah) – a tiny dinosaur that walked on all fours and probably had long, fern-like spines on its back, which may have been used for gliding.

Lystrosaurus (list-roh-sor-us) – a heavily built herbivore about the size of a pig. It walked on all fours, nesting in burrows dug out with its powerful front legs. Instead of teeth it had two tusks.

Millipede (mill-ee-peed) – Triassic millipedes were very similar to those living today. They were long creatures with many pairs of legs and a protective external skeleton. They didn't hunt, their main diet being moss, and they were good at burrowing head-first into the ground.

Plateosaurus (plat-ee-oh-sor-us) – a large, heavily built dinosaur with a very small head. It could rear up on its back legs and had a long neck so it could reach into trees and eat the leaves.

Postosuchus (poss-toh-suck-us) – this 4–5 metre long creature wasn't a dinosaur, but a close ancestor of today's crocodiles. Unlike crocodiles, its legs were tucked under its body and it had protective plates on its backs. It had large, sharp teeth and hunted its food.

Triassic (try-as-sick) – from about 200 to 250 million years ago, during this time period, seed plants and spiney trees flourished on land along with many species of reptiles and, eventually, the first dinosaurs.

Get out of our way!
We're coming through …